Don't tell Rob and Courtney
this book is dedicated to them

A FEIWEL AND FRIENDS BOOK
An imprint of Macmillan Publishing Group, LLC
175 Fifth Avenue, New York, NY 10010

Printed in China by RR Donnelley Asia Printing Solutions Ltd., Dongguan City, Guangdong Province.

Our books may be purchased in bulk for promotional, educational, or business use.
Please contact your local bookseller or the Macmillan Corporate and Premium Sales Department
at (800) 221-7945 ext. 5442 or by e-mail at MacmillanSpecialMarkets@macmillan.com.

Library of Congress Cataloging-in-Publication Data
Names: Booth, Tom, 1983— author, illustrator.
Title: Don't tell! / Tom Booth. | Other titles: Do not tell!
Description: First edition. | New York: Feiwel and Friends, 2018. | Summary: A group of
animals tries to find out who told the reader about this book, which is "super-duper secret."
Identifiers: LCCN 2017042034 | ISBN 9781250117373 (hardcover)
Subjects: | CYAC: Books—Fiction. | Secrets—Fiction. | Animals—Fiction.
Classification: LCC PZ7.1.B66814 Dt 2018 | DDC [E]—dc23
LC record available at https://lccn.loc.gov/2017042034

Book design by Tom Booth, Rich Deas, Eileen Savage, and Carol Ly

Feiwel and Friends logo designed by Filomena Tuosto

First edition, 2018

The artwork was created using a combination of traditional and digital techniques.
Tom begins by illustrating characters and environments in ink,
graphite, charcoal, or gouache. He then scans those early sketches
so he can redraw and refine his illustrations in the computer,
using digital brushes and other tools in Photoshop.

1 3 5 7 9 10 8 6 4 2

mackids.com

Author's Note

Many children tell and keep secrets with and from friends and relatives,
and most of the time, this activity is innocent and safe, as is portrayed in this book.

However, it is important for adults to talk to children about how to judge the difference between
secrets that are harmless and those that should be shared with a caregiver or teacher.

DON'T TELL!

TOM BOOTH

Feiwel and Friends
New York

How did you find this book?
Don't you know this book is a secret book?

Maybe
Frog told.

Maybe
Pig told.

Maybe
Giraffe told.

Maybe
Bear told.

I wonder
who it was . . .

Hey, everyone, do you want to hear a SECRET?

Maybe later, Harvey.
We're trying to figure out
who told this kid about
our super-secret book.

Oh.

Who, me?
Um . . .
well . . .

Harvey . . .

See, the
thing is . . .

It was ME!

I told this kid about this super-duper-secret book!

I guess I like to share secrets more than I like to keep them.

Oh, what's wrong with me?!

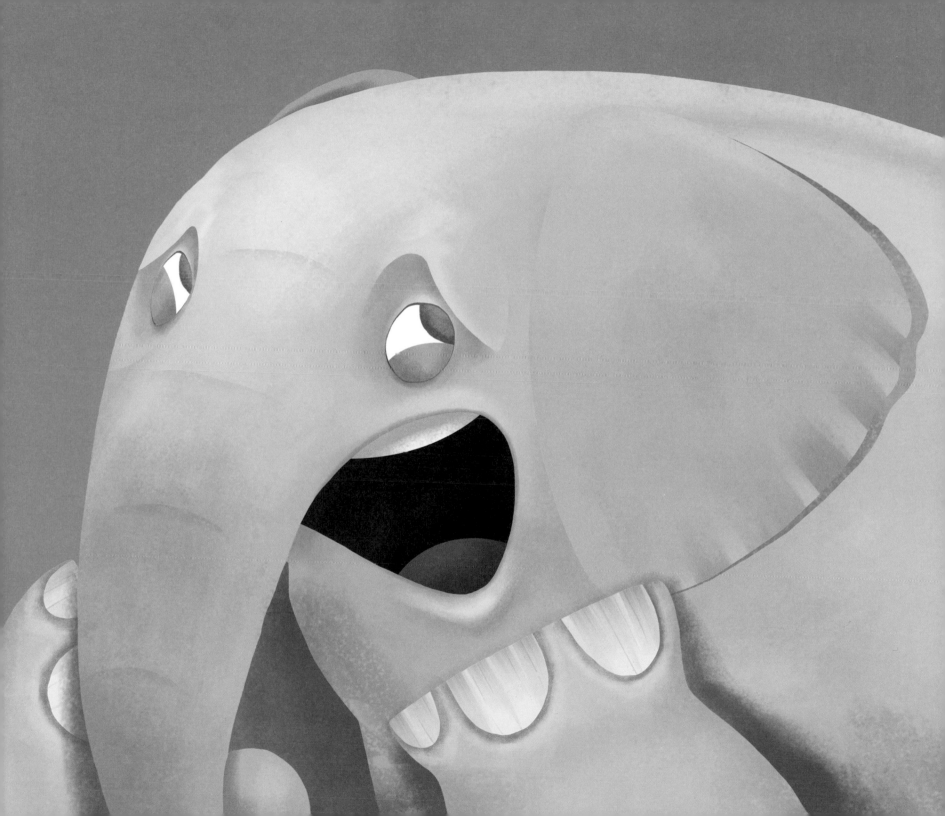

I'm sorry, everyone. I'm not very good at keeping secrets.

It's okay, Harvey!

Me too.

Me too.

Me too.

Me too.